This book has been endorsed by
CHILDHELP USA,
the largest national, nonprofit organization
dedicated to the research, prevention,
and treatment of child abuse.
1-800-4ACHILD

With love always to
Jordan, Lindsay, Noël, and Nelson.
Thank you for your inspiration and support.

ISBN: 0-7871-1041-8

Printed in the United States of America

A Dove Kids Book
A Division of Dove Audio
8955 Beverly Boulevard
West Hollywood, CA 90048

Distributed by Penguin USA

Jacket design by Rick Penn-Kraus

Type design and layout by Carolyn Wendt

First printing: September 1996

10 9 8 7 6 5 4 3 2 1

The Adventures of Little Nettie Windship

Written by

Cheryl Ladd
Brian Russell

Illustrated by

Ezra Tucker
Nancy Krause

DOVE KIDS

It was a bright and cheerful morning in the busy harbor. The great ships and the little boats happily tooted good morning to each other as they set off for work.

It was an especially exciting day for Little Nettie Windship as she sat high on top of a launching slip looking down at the sparkling blue water. Although she was excited, Little Nettie was also kind of nervous. It looked like a very long, slippery slide down to the water, and she'd never done anything like this before.

Suddenly Nettie felt something heavy on the top of her shiny new mast. As she rolled her eyes up to examine what it could possibly be, she heard . . . "Harrrrumph!" Nettie could see it was a big white bird with a huge pouchy beak. He cleared his throat to speak. "Harrrrumph!" he began. "I can see you look frightfully nervous, my dear, and I'd like to help you in any way I can."

Nettie *was* still a bit nervous, but she was so grateful to have a new friend. "Thank you very much," Nettie said, "but may I ask who are you?"

The bird smiled down at Nettie and introduced himself. "Periwinkle H. Pelican at your service. The watch bird of the harbor. I have a bird's-eye view, you might say. I've come to tell you not to be afraid.

"Why, even little baby ducklings do this all the time. The water's great! You'll love it!"

With that, Perry rose gracefully into the sky and did a perfect swan dive into the blue ocean. With a wink, he beckoned to Nettie.

Nettie took a deep breath, closed her eyes, and pushed off.
She couldn't bear to look. She began to slide, faster and faster,
down toward the water.

With a great splash, Little Nettie wooshed into the warm water
and bobbed there in the gentle breeze.

Slowly she opened her eyes and smiled to herself at how silly she'd been. The water *was* wonderful!

The baby ducklings cheered and cheered. "We knew you could do it!" they quacked.

Suddenly a furry head popped up from under the launching slip and grumbled angrily at Nettie. "Hey there, you! Whadda ya think you're doin'? You shouldn't 'otta' done that, you know. Somebody might live here, you know. Somebody 'otta' have been taking his nap, you know."

"Oh, I'm frightfully sorry, sir," said Little Nettie. "I didn't know anyone lived here. I didn't mean to disturb you. It's just that I'm new here and—"

"Well, it 'otta' never happen again," grouched the otter. "And just who are you, anyway?"

"I'm Little Nettie Windship. What's your name?"

Just then, Perry soared close by and teased, "Oh, don't mind that bully. Come on, Nettie, let me show you around. Over here you can see—"

"Hey, wait!" said the otter. "Nobody can show her the harbor like Ottwell J. Otter can. After all, I know this place like the back of my tail. Besides, I 'otta' make sure that ya stay outta trouble."

So off the new friends went: Ottie Otter, Perry Pelican, and Little Nettie Windship. As they explored, Nettie saw lots of different kinds of boats and creatures she'd never seen before. A little porpoise bobbed her head and squeaked with excitement as the new boat sailed by. It was a bright and beautiful calm day, and Nettie was having oodles of fun.

All of a sudden, from out of nowhere, a great black cloud started
to appear. Soon the entire harbor was filled with thick smelly smoke.
Somewhere, way in the middle of the cloud, Little Nettie could just
barely see the outline of the filthiest boat she'd ever seen. The tramp
steamer coughed and wheezed as he lumbered through the harbor, his
decks piled high with garbage. He was old and rusty and looked very
sad. As he trudged on he didn't seem to notice as pieces of trash fell
off into the water. It was as if he didn't care.

Ottie looked disgusted. "Hey," he said, "it's that old tramp steamer foulin' up the whole works again. Somebody 'otta' do somethin' about him, you know."

With that, Perry Pelican began to dive into the water to gather up as much of the garbage as possible.

As the three friends watched, something amazing happened. The cloud of smoke was so thick that the steamer couldn't see where he was going. He couldn't see that he was headed straight for the pier. With a loud thud, he smashed into the big wooden pier and began to list over on his side. Somehow he'd gotten himself well and truly stuck and couldn't get loose, no matter how hard he steamed.

Nettie quickly realized that the boat was in deep trouble. There was a hole in his side and the tide was rising! Soon the sea would rush in and the steamer would sink to the very bottom. Nettie called out to her friends. "Quick!" she cried. "We've got to help him."

"Not me," said Ottie. "This is just what that smelly old tub deserves."

"Oh, dear, no," said Perry. "I think that the only sensible course to take would be to arrange a meeting of—"

"Oh, please," Nettie pleaded. "I'm so sorry for interrupting, but we must waste no time. He'll drown if we don't do something."

"Well, well, now," said Perry, "what could we possibly do? Merely consider the size of that vessel and then look at us. Why, it's scientifically impossible for us to even consider—"

"Oh, please, Perry, oh, please, Ottie, we've got to at least try. We're the only chance he's got."

"Well, all right," said Perry, "but I must insist that we proceed—"

"Well, okay," said Ottie, "but I 'otta' say, Nettie, you're kinda pushy for a newcomer, you know."

"Oh, thank you," said Nettie. "Now, Ottie, I need you to grab my net and swim it over to Steamer. Tie it to him just as tight as you can. And you, Perry, take this rope and be ready when I say go." When everything was set, Nettie counted to three, and all together they began to pull as hard as they could.

They huffed and puffed and flapped and strained and heaved and ho'd, but no matter how hard they tried, Tramp Steamer just wouldn't budge. As they were just about to give up, so tired they could pull no more, Little Nettie's sail began to flap gently. In just a few moments her little sail was full of fresh wind, and she began to feel new strength.

"Come on," she cried, "we can do it!" They all three pulled again as hard as they could. Tramp Steamer began to tremble ever so slightly.

Slowly, slowly he began to move. At the same exact
moment the tide rose just enough to help.

The three friends cheered and cheered as Tramp Steamer once again floated free. "Thank you, oh, thank you," he wheezed. "If it hadn't been for your help, I'd a' been a dead duck. Tell you what," gasped Steamer gratefully, "if there's anything I can ever do for you three, don't be afraid to ask. It's been such a long time since I've had any friends, you know . . . but you all seem so very nice."

"Well," said Little Nettie, "there is something we'd like to talk to you about. It has to do with cleaning up your act. . . ."

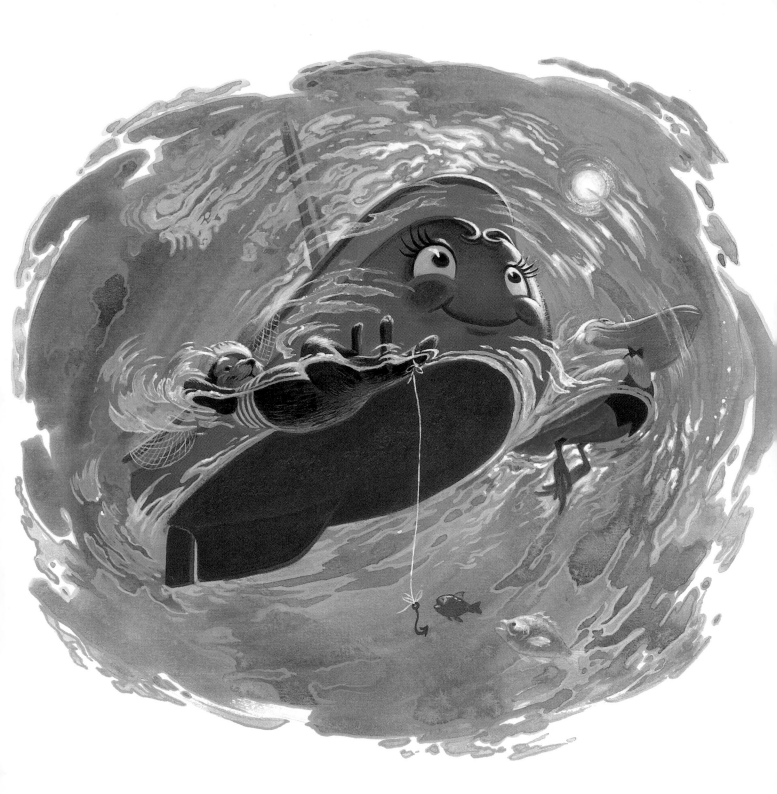

Some days later, as Little Nettie, Perry Pelican, and Ottie Otter drifted lazily on the tide, their attention was focused on the great gray doors across the way. A sign above the vast doors said:

NOAH SHARK
DRY DOCTOR
REFIT FOR A KING

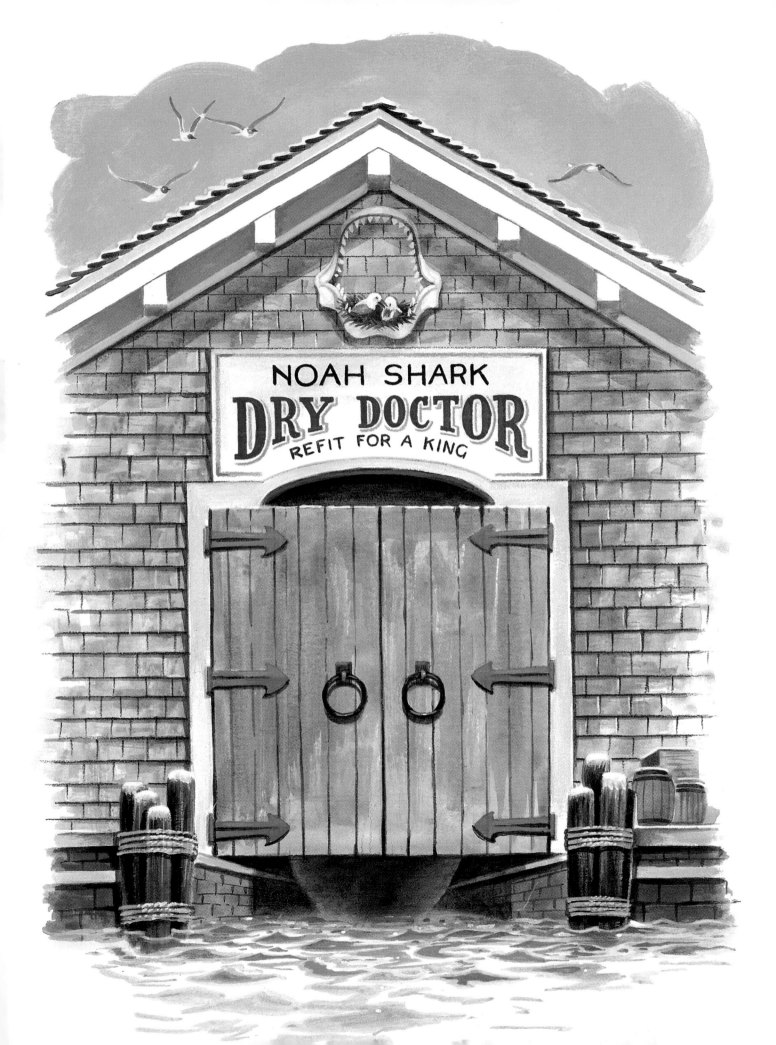

Suddenly the great doors began to grind open. The three friends watched in disbelief as a very elegant ship floated out into the harbor. They were amazed. Steamer looked so pleased with himself and his new fittings and paint. There was no more smoke belching from his stack. His new engine hummed like a dream.

Nettie was so happy she could have cried. Ottie was shaking his head in wonder. Perry was actually speechless. Little Nettie Windship gently sailed up close to Steamer. She looked up at him admiringly and smiled. "Tramp Steamer," she said, "we're all so proud of your positive changes for the good of all that we've decided to change your name to match. From now on you shall be known as . . .

Good
Citizen*ship*."